Pout-Pout Fish
Lucky Leprechaun

Written by **Wes Adams**   Illustrated by **Isidre Monés**

Based on the *New York Times*–bestselling Pout-Pout Fish books
written by Deborah Diesen and illustrated by Dan Hanna

SCHOLASTIC INC.

ISBN 978-1-338-66230-6

12 11 10 9 8 7 6 5 4 3   20 21 22 23 24 25

Printed in the U.S.A.   40

First Scholastic printing, February 2020

Designed by Aram Kim

Every St. Patrick's Day, Mr. Fish dresses up in a tall hat and whiskers and carries a pot of gold. But this year his pot is empty.

"What a wonderful leprechaun costume!" says Miss Shimmer.
"But my golden treasure is missing," Mr. Fish says. "Leprechauns always carry a pot of gold."

"We'll find it," says his friend. "Wearing green on St. Patrick's Day should bring us all good luck."

Mrs. Squid spreads the word.
"We're looking for the missing treasure," she says.

"Missing treasure?"
echoes Ms. Clam. "Oh my."

Besides his treasure, Mr. Fish has also lost his holiday cheer.

"We must find the missing gold!" declares Mr. Eight.

Up and down, over and under, the creatures
follow one another through the sea.

As they parade after the missing treasure, a worried Pout-Pout Fish leads the way.

...neath the Emerald Isle,
...cited searchers scatter
...very direction.

"If you were golden treasure,
where would you hide?"
Mr. Fish wonders.

"In the big-big dark," says Mr. Lantern.
"Let's see what we can find."

Mr. Lantern and a nervous Mr. Fish swim down, down, down, where they discover a wild array of creatures—but not Mr. Fish's special treasure.

Mr. Fish is glad to leave the depths behind.

No luck! Lounging on a sandy bed near the Sham-Rock, the Oysters explain that they only know about hiding pearls inside their shells. Mr. Fish's smile goes further upside down.

"How about the shipwreck?" says Mr. Eight.

In the hold of a sunken pirate ship, they find a chest of golden coins. "Is this the treasure you are looking for?" asks Ms. Clam.

"No," says Mr. Fish.
"I'm going home," says a disappointed
searcher, heading toward Rainbow Reef.

As Mr. Fish watches the small fish swim away, he has an idea.
"I think I know where my treasure is!" He darts off, and the others follow.

At the end of Rainbow Reef, in a hidden
hollow, Mr. Fish finds what he is seeking:
a school of shimmering yellow butterfly fish.
"We've found the gold at the end of the
rainbow!" Mr. Eight declares.

"We thought it would be fun to play hide-and-seek," say the mischievous golden fish as they swirl back into Mr. Fish's pot, completing his costume.

It is a happy parade home, now that Mr. Fish is reunited
with his little friends.

"What a lucky day!" says a smiling Mr. Fish.
"HAPPY ST. PATRICK'S DAY TO ONE AND ALL!"